To my dearest friends who support me endlessly,
and to my fellow Pam Beeslys out there:
"Be strong. Trust yourself. Love yourself. Conquer your fears.
Just go after what you want, and act fast,
because life just isn't that long." —M. D.

To my office mates who made work fun:
"I wish there was a way to know you're in the good old days,
before you've actually left them." —R. P.

Little, Brown and Company
Hachette Book Group
1290 Avenue of the Americas, New York, NY 10104
Visit us at LBYR.com

First Edition: September 2020

Little, Brown and Company is a division of Hachette Book Group, Inc. The Little, Brown name and logo are trademarks of Hachette Book Group, Inc.

The publisher is not responsible for websites (or their content) that are not owned by the publisher.

ISBNs: 978-0-316-42838-5 (hardcover), 978-0-316-42839-2 (ebook), 978-0-316-42840-8 (ebook), 978-0-316-42843-9 (ebook)

Printed in China

APS

10 9 8 7 6 5 4 3 2 1

the office

A Day at Dunder Mifflin Elementary

MICHAEL

PAM

JIM

DWIGHT

WELCOME TO MS. LEVINSON'S CLASS!

Can you find all these things as you read the story?

Pretzel

Kelly's Birthday Mugs

Stanley's Crossword

Pam's Office Painting

Beet Plants

The Dundie Award

Sprinkles, Angela's Cat

Stapler in Gelatin

Dwight Bobblehead

World's Best Boss Mug

Schrute Bucks

Bob Vance, Vance Refrigeration

the office
A Day at Dunder Mifflin Elementary

Written by
Robb Pearlman

Illustrated by
Melanie Demmer

Little, Brown and Company

New York Boston

I'm Michael Scott. I'm a student at Dunder Mifflin Elementary. When Principal Wallace and Ms. Levinson asked me to be the class Line Leader, I told them I needed two days before I could start...

...because that's how long it took my mom to get *this* made. Now everyone will know I'm the World's Best Line Leader!

WORLD'S BEST LINE LEADER

SCHRUTE FARM BEETS

MUNG BEANS

"This class is a mess, Michael!" Dwight complains. "You should let someone help you be Line Leader."

"I don't need help. I can do it by myself," I say.

"For real, Michael?"
Kelly butts in.
"Please. You need all
the help you can get,"
Stanley adds.

"Fine. You can be the Assistant to the
Line Leader," I tell Dwight so everyone will
stop bugging me. I don't *really* need help.

"Assistant Line Leader! I accept," he says.
"Assistant *to* the Line Leader," I correct
him. I'm going to show this class that I am
the World's Best Line Leader. "It's time for a
meeting!" I yell.

"Come on, everyone," Dwight says. "Nice and orderly!"

"Yeah, nice and orderly! *Rit dit dit dit doo!*" adds Andy.

"But I have math to learn!" complains Oscar.

"A mistake plus Keleven equals seven!" says Kevin.

"Meetings are fun," says Erin. "What are meetings like?"

Once the class is settled, I make my announcement:
"I will lead my first line into a big party. Angela, can
you throw one in five minutes?"

"Plan a party in only five minutes?" she asks.
"Ryan, Phyllis, and Meredith, you can help," I suggest.
"Do you really think this is a good idea?" asks Ryan.
"Of course it's a good idea!" I say. "Parties are always a good idea!"

I just hope *this* party is better than my last birthday party. I was allergic to the pony my mom rented and had to spend the whole day inside.

WORLD'S BEST LINE LEADER

AH-CHOO

After I end the meeting, Dwight has even more questions for me.

"Michael, *how* are we going to line up for the party? Order is very important. The first person gets all the good snacks. And you know what it's like to be last!"

"I have a plan!" I tell him.

"Ummm," I say, and look around the room.
"What if we line up alphabetically?"

Aa Bb Cc Dd Ee Ff Gg Hh Ii Jj Kk Ll Mm Nn

"Actually..." Oscar starts to say.
"We haven't all learned the alphabet yet,"
Toby adds.
"Everyone, line up!" I declare.

But our first line is not right at all.
"This is not alphabetical!" I shout.

So then I have the class line up shortest to tallest,
but *that* doesn't work because Kelly's legs are little.
She doesn't walk as fast as everyone else.

Tallest to shortest doesn't work, either, because Dwight can't see around Kevin's head.

Being a Line Leader is hard!

Next, I have the class race so they can line up from fastest to slowest. I try to get Stanley to run, but he doesn't listen.

Ugh! Nothing works. Not even the paper airplane-throwing contest. What am I going to do? They're all going to think I'm the World's *Worst* Line Leader!

Just when I think I'll have to cancel the party, Pam asks me, "You okay, Michael?"

"You bet!" I reply. "I just...don't know what to do."

"My mom taught me you should ask for help when you need it," Pam says. "Everyone, even Line Leaders, needs to ask for help sometimes."

"Whoa. Pam, your mom is an amazing lady," I say.

"Attention, Dunder Mifflin Elementary! Everyone, even Line Leaders like me, needs to ask for help sometimes."
"Fact!" Dwight declares.

"So please help me be the World's Best Line Leader," I say. "How do *you* want to line up?"

The class has amazing ideas, but I choose the Buddy System!

Everyone holds hands with a buddy, and
it works! The class is in a great line!
"Way to go, Line Leader," Jim says.
"That was a really good choice, Michael,"
Darryl says.

"As Assistant Line Leader,
I agree!" Dwight declares.
   "Assistant *to* the Line Leader,"
I tell him with a smile.

I'm Michael Scott. I'm a Line Leader at Dunder Mifflin Elementary. And I lead a great class.